THE DOOR

into Infinity

THE DOOR

into Infinity

EDMOND HAMILTON

ÆGYPAN PRESS

From *Weird Tales,* August–September 1936.

Special thanks to Greg Weeks, Mary Meehan, and the Online
Distributed Proofreading Team (which can be found at
http://www.pgdp.net).

The Door into Infinity
A publication of
ÆGYPAN PRESS

www.aegypan.com

An amazing weird mystery story, packed with thrills, danger, and startling events.

I

The Brotherhood of the Door

"*W*here leads the Door?"
"*It leads outside our world.*"
"Who taught our forefathers to open the Door?"
"*They Beyond the Door taught them.*"
"To whom do we bring these sacrifices?"
"*We bring them to Those Beyond the Door.*"
"Shall the Door be opened that They may take them?"
"*Let the Door be opened!*"

Paul Ennis had listened thus far, his haggard face uncomprehending in expression, but now he interrupted the speaker.

"But what does it all mean, inspector? Why are you repeating this to me?"

"Did you ever hear anyone speak words like that?" asked Inspector Pierce Campbell, leaning tautly forward for the answer.

"Of course not – it just sounds like gibberish to me," Ennis exclaimed. "What connection can it have with my wife?"

He had risen to his feet, a tall, blond young American whose good-looking face was drawn and worn by inward agony, whose crisp yellow hair was brushed back from his forehead in disorder, and whose blue eyes were haunted with an anguished dread.

He kicked back his chair and strode across the gloomy little office, whose single window looked out on the thickening, foggy twilight of London. He bent across the dingy desk, gripping its edges with his hands as he spoke tensely to the man sitting behind it.

"Why are we wasting time talking here?" Ennis cried. "Sitting here talking, when anything may be happening to Ruth!

"It's been hours since she was kidnapped. They may have taken her anywhere, even outside of London by now. And instead of searching for her, you sit here and talk gibberish about Doors!"

Inspector Campbell seemed unmoved by Ennis' passion. A bulky, almost bald man, he looked up with his colorless, sagging face, in which his eyes gleamed like two crumbs of bright brown glass.

"You're not helping me much by giving way to your emotions, Mr. Ennis," he said in his flat voice.

"Give way? Who wouldn't give way?" cried Ennis. "Don't you understand, man, it's Ruth that's gone — my wife! Why, we were married only last week in New York. And on our second day here in London, I see her whisked into a limousine and carried away before my eyes! I thought you men at Scotland Yard here would surely act, do something. Instead you talk crazy gibberish to me!"

"Those words are *not* gibberish," said Pierce Campbell quietly. "And I think they're related to the abduction of your wife."

"What do you mean? How could they be related?"

The inspector's bright little brown eyes held Ennis'. "Did you ever hear of an organization called the Brotherhood of the Door?"

Ennis shook his head, and Campbell continued, "Well, I am certain your wife was kidnapped by members of the Brotherhood."

"What kind of an organization is it?" the young American demanded. "A band of criminals?"

"No, it is no ordinary criminal organization," the detective said. His sagging face set strangely. "Unless I am mistaken, the Brotherhood of the Door is the most unholy and blackly evil organization that has ever existed on this earth. Almost nothing is known of it outside its circle. I myself in twenty years have learned little except its existence and name. That ritual I just repeated to you, I heard from the lips of a dying member of the Brotherhood, who repeated the words in his delirium."

Campbell leaned forward. "But I know that every year about this time the Brotherhood come from all over the world and gather at some secret center here in England. And every year, before that gathering, scores of people are kidnapped and never heard of again. I believe that all those people are kidnapped by this mysterious Brotherhood."

"But what becomes of the people they kidnap?" cried the pale young American. "What do they do with them?"

*I*nspector Campbell's bright brown eyes showed a hint of hooded horror, yet he shook his head. "I know no more than you. But whatever they do to the victims, they are never heard of again."

"But you must know something more!" Ennis protested. "What is this Door?"

Campbell again shook his head. "That too I don't know, but whatever it is, the Door is utterly sacred to the members of the Brotherhood, and whomever they mean by They Beyond the Door, they dread and venerate to the utmost."

"Where leads the Door? *It leads outside our world,*" repeated Ennis. "What can that mean?"

"It might have a symbolic meaning, referring to some secluded fastness of the order which is away from the rest of the world," the inspector said. "Or it might —"

He stopped. "Or it might what?" pressed Ennis, his pale face thrust forward.

"It might mean, literally, that the Door leads outside our world and universe," finished the inspector.

Ennis' haunted eyes stared. "You mean that this Door might somehow lead into another universe? But that's impossible!"

"Perhaps unlikely," Campbell said quietly, "but not impossible. Modern science has taught us that there are other universes than the one we live in, universes congruent and coincident with our own in space and time, yet separated from our own by the impassable barrier of totally different dimensions. It is not entirely impossible that a greater science than ours might find a way to pierce that barrier between our universe and one of those outside ones, that a Door should be opened from ours into one of those others in the infinite outside."

"A door into the infinite outside," repeated Ennis broodingly, looking past the inspector. Then he made a sudden movement of wild impatience, the dread leaping back strong in his eyes again.

"Oh, what good is all this talk about Doors and infinite universes doing in finding Ruth? I want to *do* something! If you think this mysterious Brotherhood has taken her, you must surely have some idea of how we can get her back from them? You must know something more about them than you've told."

"I don't know anything more certainly, but I've certain suspicions that amount to convictions," Inspector Campbell said. "I've been working on this Brotherhood for many years, and block after block I've narrowed down to the place I think the order's local center, the London headquarters of the Brotherhood of the Door."

"Where is the place?" asked Ennis tensely.

"It is the waterfront café of one Chandra Dass, a Hindu, down by East India Docks," said the detective officer. "I've been there in disguise more than once, watching the place. This Chandra Dass I've found to be immensely feared by everyone in the quarter, which strengthens my belief that he's one of the high officers of the Brotherhood. He's too exceptional a man to be really running such a place."

"Then if the Brotherhood took Ruth, she may be at that place now!" cried the young American, electrified.

Campbell nodded his bald head. "She may very likely be. Tonight I'm going there again in disguise, and have men ready to raid the place. If Chandra Dass has your wife there, we'll get her before he can get her away. Whatever way it turns out, we'll let you know at once."

"Like hell you will!" exploded the pale young Ennis. "Do you think I'm going to twiddle my thumbs while you're down there? I'm going with you. And if you refuse to let me, by heaven I'll go there myself!"

Inspector Pierce Campbell gave the haggard, fiercely determined face of the young man a long look, and then his own colorless countenance seemed to soften a little.

"All right," he said quietly. "I can disguise you so you'll not be recognized. But you'll have to follow my orders exactly, or death will result for both of us."

That strange, hooded dread flickered again in his eyes, as though he saw through shrouding mists the outline of dim horror.

"It may be," he added slowly, "that something worse even than death awaits those who try to oppose the Brotherhood of the Door — something that would explain the unearthly, superhuman dread that enwraps the secret mysteries of the order. We're taking more than our lives in our hands, I think, in trying to unveil those mysteries, to regain your wife. But we've got to act quickly, at all costs. We've got to find her before the great gathering of the Brotherhood takes place, or we'll never find her."

*T*wo hours before midnight found Campbell and Ennis passing along a cobble-paved waterfront street north of the great East India Docks. Big warehouses towered black and silent in the darkness on one side, and on the other were old, rotting docks beyond which Ennis glimpsed the black water and gliding lights of the river.

As they straggled beneath the infrequent lights of the ill-lit street, they were utterly changed in appearance. Inspector Campbell, dressed in a shabby suit and rusty bowler, his dirty white shirt innocent of tie, had acquired a new face, a bright red, oily, eager one, and a high, squeaky voice. Ennis wore a rough blue seaman's jacket and a vizored cap pulled down over his head. His unshaven-looking face and subtly altered features made him seem a half-intoxicated seaman off his ship, as he stumbled unsteadily along. Campbell clung to him in true land-shark fashion, plucking his arm and talking wheedlingly to him.

They came into a more populous section of the evil old waterfront street, and passed fried-fish shops giving off the strong smell of hot fat, and the dirty, lighted windows of a half-dozen waterfront saloons, loud with sordid argument or merriment.

Campbell led past them until they reached one built upon an abandoned, moldering pier, a ramshackle frame structure extending some distance back out on the pier. Its window was curtained, but dull red light glowed through the glass window of the door.

A few shabby men were lounging in front of the place but Campbell paid them no attention, tugging Ennis inside by the arm.

"Carm on in!" he wheedled shrilly. "The night ain't 'alf over yet — we'll 'ave just one more."

"Don't want anymore," muttered Ennis drunkenly, swaying on his feet inside. "Get away, you damned old shark."

Yet he suffered himself to be led by Campbell to a table, where he slumped heavily into a chair. His stare swung vacantly.

The café of Chandra Dass was a red-lit, smoke-filled cave with cheap black curtains on the walls and windows, and other curtains cutting off the back part of the building from view. The dim room was jammed with tables crowded with patrons whose babel of tongues made an unceasing din, to which a three-string guitar somewhere added a wailing undertone. The waiters were dark-skinned and tiger-footed Malays, while the patrons seemed drawn from every nation east and west.

Ennis' glazed eyes saw dandified Chinese from Limehouse and Pennyfields, dark little Levantins from Soho, rough-looking Cockneys in shabby caps, a few crazily laughing blacks. From sly white faces, taut brown ones and impassive yellow ones came a dozen different languages. The air was thick with queer food-smells and the acrid smoke.

Campbell had selected a table near the back curtain, and now stridently ordered one of the Malay waiters to bring gin. He leaned forward with an oily smile to the drunken-looking Ennis, and spoke to him in a wheedling undertone.

"Don't look for a minute, but that's Chandra Dass over in the corner, and he's watching us," he said.

Ennis shook his clutching hand away. "Damned old shark!" he muttered again.

He turned his swaying head slowly, letting his eyes rest a moment on the man in the corner. That man was looking straight at him.

Chandra Dass was tall, dressed in spotless white from his shoes to the turban on his head. The white made his dark, impassive, aquiline face stand out in chiseled relief. His eyes were coal-black, large, coldly searching, as they met Ennis' bleared gaze.

Ennis felt a strange chill as he met those eyes. There was something alien and unhuman, something uncannily disturbing, behind the Hindu's stare. He turned his gaze vacantly from Chandra Dass to the black curtains at the rear, and then back to his companion.

The silent Malay waiter had brought the liquor, and Campbell pressed a glass toward his companion. "'Ere, matey, take this."

"Don't want it," muttered Ennis, pushing it away. Still in the same mutter, he added, "If Ruth's here, she's somewhere in the back there. I'm going back and find out."

"Don't try it that way, for God's sake!" said Campbell in the wheedling undertone. "Chandra Dass is still watching, and those Malays would be on you in a minute. Wait until I give the word.

"All right, then," Campbell added in a louder, injured tone. "If you don't want it, I'll drink it myself."

He tossed off the glass of gin and set the glass down on the table, looking at his drunken companion with righteous indignation.

"Think I'm tryin' to bilk yer, eh?" he added. "That's a fine way to treat a pal!"

He added in the coaxing lower tone, "All right, I'm going to try it. Be ready to move when I light my cigarette."

He fished a soiled package of Gold Flakes from his pocket and put one in his mouth. Ennis waited, every muscle taut.

The inspector, his red, oily face still injured in expression, struck a match to his cigarette. Almost at once there was a loud oath from one of the shabby loungers outside the front of the building, and the sound of angry voices and blows.

The patrons of Chandra Dass looked toward the door, and one of the Malay waiters went hastily out to quiet the fight. But it grew swiftly, sounded in a moment like a small riot. *Crash* — someone was pushed through the front window. The excited patrons pressed toward the front. Chandra Dass pushed through them, issuing quick orders to his servants.

For the time being the back of the café was deserted and unnoticed. Campbell sprang to his feet, and with Ennis close behind him, darted through the black curtains. They found themselves in a black corridor at the end of which a red bulb burned dimly. They could still hear the uproar.

Campbell's gun was in his hand, and the American's in his.

"We dare only stay here a few moments," the inspector cried. "Look in those rooms along the corridor here."

Ennis frantically tore open a door and peered into a dark room smelling of drugs. "Ruth!" he cried softly. "Ruth!"

II

Death Trap

*T*here was no answer. The light in the corridor behind him suddenly went out, plunging him into pitch-black darkness. He jumped back into the dark corridor, and as he did so, heard a sudden scuffle further along it.

"Campbell!" he exclaimed, lunging forward in the black passageway. There was no answer.

He pitched forward through stygian obscurity, his hands searching ahead of him for the inspector. In the dark something whipped smoothly around his throat, tightened there like a slender, contracting tentacle.

Ennis tore frenziedly at the thing, which he felt to be a slender silken cord, but he could not loosen it. It was choking him. He tried to cry out again to Campbell, but his throat could not emit the sounds. He thrashed, twisted helplessly, hearing a loud roaring in his ears, consciousness receding. Then, dimly as though in a dream, Ennis was aware of being lowered to the floor, of being half carried and half dragged along. The constriction around his throat was gone and rapidly his brain began to clear. He opened his eyes.

He found himself lying on the floor of a room illuminated by a great hanging brass lamp of ornate design. The walls of the room were hung with rich, grotesquely worked red silk Indian draperies. His hands and feet were bound behind him, and beside him, tied in the same manner, lay Inspector Campbell. Over them stood Chandra Dass and two of the Malay servants. The faces of the servants were tigerish in their menace, but Chandra Dass' face was one of dark, impassive scorn.

"So you misguided fools thought you could deceive me so easily as that?" he said in a strong, vibrant voice. "Why, we knew hours ago that you, Inspector Campbell, and you, Mr. Ennis, were coming here tonight. We let you get this far only because it was evident that somehow you had learned too much about us, and that it would be best to let you come here and meet your deaths."

"Chandra Dass, I've men outside," rasped Campbell. "If we don't come out, they'll come in after us."

The Hindu's proud, dark face did not change its scorn. "They will not come in for a little while, inspector. By that time you two will be dead and we shall be gone with our captives. Yes, Mr. Ennis, your wife is one of those captives," he added to the prostrate young American. "It is too bad we cannot take you and the inspector to share her glorious destiny, but then our accommodations of transport are limited."

"Ruth here?" Ennis' face flamed at the words, and he raised himself a little from the floor on his elbows.

"Then you'll let her go if I pay you? I'll raise any amount, I'll do anything you ask, if you'll set her free."

"No amount of money in the world could buy her from the Brotherhood of the Door," answered Chandra Dass steadily. "For she belongs now, not to us, but to They Beyond the Door. Within a few hours she and many others shall stand before the Door, and They Beyond the Door shall take them."

"What are you going to do to her?" cried Ennis. "What is this damned Door and who are They Beyond it?"

"I do not think that even if I told you, your little mind would be able to accept the mighty truth," Chandra Dass said calmly. His coal-black eyes suddenly flashed with fanatic, frenetic light. "How could your poor, earth-bound little intelligences conceive the true nature of the Door and of those who dwell beyond it? Your puny brains would be stricken senseless by mere apprehension of them, They who are mighty and crafty and dreadful beyond anything on earth."

A cold wind from the alien unknown seemed to sweep the lamplit room with the Hindu's passionate words. Then that rapt, fanatic exaltation dropped from him as suddenly as it had come, and he spoke in his ordinary vibrant tones.

"But enough of this parley with blind worms of the dust. Bring the weights!"

The last words were addressed to the Malay servants, who sprang to a closet in the corner of the room.

Inspector Campbell said steadily, "If my men find us dead when they come in here, they'll leave none of you living."

Chandra Dass did not even listen to him, but ordered the dark servants sharply, "Attach the weights!"

The Malays had brought from the closet two fifty-pound lead balls, and now they proceeded quickly to tie these to the feet of the two men. Then one of them rolled back the brilliant red Indian rug from the rough pine floor. A square trapdoor was disclosed, and at Chandra Dass' order, it was swung upward and open.

Up through the open square came the sound of waves slap-slapping against the piles of the old pier, and the heavy odors of salt water and of rotting wood invaded the room.

"The water under this pier is twenty feet deep," Chandra Dass told the two prisoners. "I regret to give you so easy a death, but there is no opportunity to take you to the fate you deserve."

Ennis, his skin crawling on his flesh, nevertheless spoke rapidly and as steadily as possible to the Hindu.

"Listen, I don't ask you to let me go, but I'll do anything you want, let you kill me any way you want, if you'll let Ruth —"

Sheer horror cut short his words. The Malay servants had dragged Campbell's bound body to the door in the floor. They shoved him over the edge. Ennis had one glimpse of the inspector's taut, strange face falling out of sight. Then a dull splash sounded instantly below, and then silence.

He felt hands upon himself, dragging him across the floor. He fought, crazily, hopelessly, twisting his body in its bonds, thrashing his bound limbs wildly.

He saw the dark, unmoved face of Chandra Dass, the brass lamp over his head, the red hangings. Then his head dangled over the opening, a shove sent his body scraping over the edge, and he plunged downward through dank darkness. With a splash he hit the icy water and went under. The heavy weight at his ankles dragged him irresistibly downward. Instinctively he held his breath as the water rushed upward around him.

His feet struck oozy bottom. His body swayed there, chained by the lead weight to the bottom. His lungs already were bursting to draw in air, slow fires seeming to creep through his breast as he held his breath.

Ennis knew that in a moment or two more he would inhale the strangling waters and die. The thought-picture of Ruth flashed across his despairing mind, wild with hopeless regret. He could no longer hold his breath, felt his muscles relaxing against his will, tasted the stinging salt water at the back of his nose.

Then it was a bursting confusion of swift sensations, the choking water in his nose and throat, the roaring in his ears. A scroll of flame unrolled slowly in his brain and a voice shouted there, "You're dying!" He felt dimly a plucking at his ankles.

Abruptly Ennis' dimming mind was aware that he now was shooting upward through the water. His head burst into open air and he choked, strangled and gasped, his tortured lungs gulping the damp, heavy air. He opened his eyes, and shook the water from them.

He was floating in the darkness at the surface of the water. Someone was floating beside him, supporting him. Ennis' chin bumped the other's shoulder, and he heard a familiar voice.

"Easy, now," said Inspector Campbell. "Wait till I cut your hands loose."

"Campbell!" Ennis choked. "How did you get loose?"

"Never mind that now," the inspector answered. "Don't make any noise, or they may hear us up there."

Ennis felt a knife-blade slashing the bonds at his wrists. Then, the inspector's arm helping him, he and his companion paddled weakly through the darkness under the rotting pier. They bumped against the slimy, moldering piles, threaded through them toward the side of the pier. The waves of the flooding tide washed them up and down as Campbell led the way.

They passed out from under the old pier into the comparative illumination of the stars. Looking back up, Ennis saw the long, black mass of the house of Chandra Dass, resting on the black pier, ruddy light glowing from window-cracks. He collided with something and found that Campbell had led toward a little floating dock where some skiffs were moored. They scrambled up onto it from the water, and lay panting for a few moments.

Campbell had something in his hand, a thin, razor-edged steel blade several inches long. Its hilt was an ordinary leather shoe-heel.

The inspector turned up one of his feet and Ennis saw that the heel was missing from that shoe. Carefully Campbell slid the steel blade beneath the shoe-sole, the heel-hilt sliding into place and seeming merely the innocent heel of the shoe.

"So that's how you got loose down in the water!" Ennis exclaimed, and the inspector nodded briefly.

"That trick's done me good service before — even with your hands tied behind your back you can get out that knife and use it. It was touch and go, though, whether I could get it out and cut myself loose in the water in time enough to free you."

Ennis gripped the inspector's shoulder. "Campbell, Ruth is in there! By heaven, we've found her and now we can get her out!"

"Right!" said the officer grimly. "We'll go around to the front and in two minutes we'll be in there with my men."

*T*hey climbed dripping to their feet, and hastened from the little floating dock up onto the shore, through the darkness to the cobbled street.

The shabbily disguised men of Inspector Campbell were not now in front of Chandra Dass' café, but lurking in the shadows across the street. They came running toward Campbell and Ennis.

"All right, we're going in there," Campbell exclaimed in steely tones. "Get Chandra Dass, whatever you do, but see that his prisoners are not harmed."

He snapped a word and one of the men handed pistols to him and to Ennis. Then they leaped toward the door of the Hindu's café, from which still streamed ruddy light and the babel of many voices.

A kick from Inspector Campbell sent the door flying inward, and they burst in with guns gleaming wickedly in the ruddy light. Ennis' face was a quivering mask of desperate resolve.

The motley patrons jumped up with yells of alarm at their entrance. The hand of a Malay waiter jerked and a thrown knife thudded into the wall beside them. Ennis yelled as he saw Chandra Dass, his dark face startled, leaping back with his servants through the black curtains.

He and Campbell drove through the squealing patrons toward the back. The Malay who had thrown the knife rushed to bar the way, another dagger uplifted. Campbell's gun coughed and the Malay reeled and stumbled. The inspector and Ennis threw themselves at the black curtains — and were dashed back.

They tore aside the black folds. A dull steel door had been lowered behind them, barring the way to the back rooms. Ennis beat crazily upon it with his pistol-butt, but it remained immovable.

"No use — we can't break that down!" yelled Campbell, over the uproar. "Outside, and around to the other end of the building!"

They burst back out through that mad-house, into the dark of the street. They started along the side of the pier toward the river-end, edging forward on a narrow ledge but inches wide. As they reached the back of the building, Ennis shouted and pointed to dark figures at the end of the pier. There were two of them, lowering shapeless, wrapped forms over the end of the pier.

"There they are!" he cried. "They've got their prisoners out there with them."

Campbell's pistol leveled, but Ennis swiftly struck it up. "No, you might hit Ruth."

He and the inspector bounded forward along the pier. Fire streaked from the dark ahead and bullets thumped the rotting boards around them.

Suddenly the loud roar of an accelerated motor drowned out all other sounds. It came from the river at the pier's end.

Campbell and Ennis reached the end in time to see a long, powerful, grey motor-boat dash out into the black obscurity of the river, and roar eastward with gathering speed.

"There they go — they're getting away!" cried the agonized young American.

Inspector Campbell cupped his hands and shouted out into the darkness, "River police, ahoy! Ahoy there!"

He rasped to Ennis. "The river police were to have a cutter here tonight. We can still catch them."

With swiftly rising roar of speeded motors, a big cutter drove in from the darkness. Its searchlight snapped on, bathing the two men on the pier in a blinding glare.

"Ahoy, there!" called a stentorian voice over the roar of the motors. "Is that Inspector Campbell?"

"Yes. Come alongside," yelled the inspector, and as the big cutter shot close to the end of the pier, its reversing propellers churning the dark water to foam, Ennis and Campbell leaped.

They landed amid unseen men in the cockpit, and as he scrambled to his feet the inspector cried, "Follow that boat that just went down-river. But no shooting!"

*W*ith thunderous drumfire from its exhausts, the cutter jerked forward so rapidly that it almost threw them from their feet again. It shot out onto the bosom of the dark river that flowed like a black sea between the banks of scattered lights that were London.

The moving lights of yachts and barges coming up-river could be seen gliding in that darkness. The captain of the cutter barked an order and one of his three men, the one crouched at the searchlight, switched its powerful beam out over the waters ahead.

In a moment it picked up a distant grey spot racing eastward on the black river, leaving a white trail of foam.

"There she is!" bawled the man at the searchlight. "She's running without lights!"

"Keep her in the searchlight," ordered the captain. "Sound our siren, and give the cutter her head."

Swaying, rocking, the cutter roared on through the darkness on the trail of that distant fleeing speck. As they raced down Blackwall Reach, the distance between the two craft had already begun to lessen.

"We're overtaking him!" cried Campbell, clutching a stanchion and peering ahead against the rush of wind and spray. "He must be making for whatever spot it is in England that is the center of the Brotherhood of the Door — but he'll never reach it."

"He said that within a few hours Ruth would go with the others through the Door!" cried Ennis, clinging beside him. "Campbell, we mustn't let them get away now!"

Pursuers and pursued flashed on down the dark, broadening river, through mazes of shipping, the cutter hanging doggedly to the motor-boat's trail. The lights of London had dropped behind and those of Tilbury now gleamed away on their left.

Bigger, stronger waves now tossed and pounded the cutter as it raced out of the river mouth toward the heaving black expanse of the sea. The Kent coast was a black blur on their right; the grey motor-boat followed it closely, grazing almost beneath the Sheerness lights.

"He's heading to round North Foreland and follow the coast south to Ramsgate or Dover," the cutter captain cried to Campbell. "But we'll catch him before he passes Margate."

The quarry was now but a quarter-mile ahead. Steadily as they roared onward the gap narrowed, until in the glare of the searchlight they could make out every detail of the powerful grey motor-boat plunging through the tossing black waves.

They saw Chandra Dass' dark face turn and look back at them, and the cutter captain raised his speaking-trumpet to his lips and shouted over the roar of motors and dash of waves.

"Stand by or we'll fire at you!"

"He won't obey," muttered Campbell between his teeth. "He knows we daren't fire with the girl in the boat."

"Yes, blast him!" exclaimed the captain. "But we'll have him in a few minutes, anyway."

The thundering chase had brought them into sight of the lights of Margate on the dark coast to their right. Now only a few hundred feet of black water separated them from the fleeing craft.

Ennis and the inspector, gripping the stanchions of the rushing cutter, saw a white figure suddenly stand erect in the boat ahead and wave its arms to them. The grey motor-boat slowed.

"It's Chandra Dass and he's signaling that he's giving up!" Ennis cried. "He's stopping!"

"By heavens, he is!" Campbell explained. "Drive alongside him, and we'll soon have the irons on him."

The cutter, its own motors hastily throttled down, shot through the water toward the slowing grey craft. Ennis saw Chandra Dass standing erect, awaiting their coming, he and the two Malays beside him holding their hands in the air. He saw a half-dozen or more white-wrapped forms in the bottom of the boat, lying motionless.

"There are their prisoners!" he cried. "Bring the boat closer so we can jump in!"

He and Campbell, their pistols out, hunched to jump as the cutter drove closer to the grey motor-boat. The sides of the two craft bumped, the motors of both idling noisily. Then before Ennis and Campbell could jump into the motor-boat, things happened with cinemalike rapidity. Two of the still white forms at the bottom of the motor-boat leaped up and like suddenly uncoiled springs shot through the air into the cutter. They were two other Malays, their dark faces flaming with fanatic light, keen daggers glinting in their upraised hands.

"'Ware a trick!" yelled Campbell. His gun barked, but the bullet missed and a dagger slit his sleeve.

The Malays, with wild, screeching yells, were laying about them with their daggers in the cutter, insanely.

"God in heaven, they're running amok!" choked the cutter captain.

His slashed neck spurting blood and his face livid, he fell. One of his men slumped coughing beside him, another victim of the crazy daggers.

III

Up the Water-Tunnel

*T*he man at the searchlight sprang for the maddened Malays, tugging at his pistol as he jumped. Before he got the weapon out, a dagger slashed his jugular and he went down gurgling in death. One of the Malays meanwhile had knocked Inspector Campbell from his feet, his knife-hand swooping down, his eyes blazing.

Ennis' gun roared and the bullet hit the Malay between the eyes. But as he slumped limply, the other fanatic was upon Ennis from the side. Before Ennis could whirl to meet him, the attacker's knife grazed down past his cheek like a brand of living fire. He was borne backward by the rush, felt the hot breath of the crazed Malay in his face, the dagger-point at his throat.

Shots roared quickly, one after another, and with each shot the Malay pressing Ennis back jerked convulsively. With the light of murderous madness fading from his eyes, he still strove to drive the dagger home into the American's throat. But a hand jerked him back and he lay prostrate and still.

Ennis scrambled up to find Inspector Campbell, pale and determined, over him. The detective had shot the attacker from behind.

The captain of the cutter and two of his men lay dead in the cockpit beside the two Malays. The remaining seaman, the helmsman, held his shoulder and groaned.

Ennis whirled. The motor-boat of Chandra Dass was no longer beside the cutter, and there was no sight of it anywhere on the black sea ahead. The Hindu had taken advantage of the fight to make good his escape with his two other servants and their prisoners.

"Campbell, he's gone!" cried the young American frantically. "He's got away!"

The inspector's eyes were bright with cold flame of anger. "Yes, Chandra Dass sacrificed these two Malays to hold us up long enough for him to escape."

Campbell whirled to the helmsman. "You're not badly hurt?"

"Only a scratch, but I nearly broke my shoulder when I fell," answered the man.

"Then head on around North Foreland!" Campbell cried. "We may still be able to catch up to them."

"But Captain Wilson and the others are killed," protested the helmsman. "I've got to report —"

"You can report later," rasped the inspector. "Do as I say — I'll be responsible."

"Very well, sir," said the helmsman, and jumped back to the wheel.

In a minute the big cutter was roaring ahead over the heaving black waves, its searchlight clawing the darkness ahead. There was no sign now of the craft of Chandra Dass ahead. They raced abreast of the lights of Margate, started rounding the North Foreland, pounded by bigger seas.

Inspector Campbell had dragged the bodies of the dead policemen and their two slayers down into the cabin of the cutter. He came up and crouched down with Ennis beside Sturt, the helmsman.

"I found these on the two Malays," Campbell shouted to the American, holding out two little objects in his spray-wet hand.

Each was a flat star of grey metal in which was set a large oval, cabochon-cut jewel. The jewels flashed and dazzled with deep color, but it was a color wholly unfamiliar and alien to their eyes.

"They're not any color we know on earth," Campbell shouted. "I believe these jewels came from somewhere beyond the Door, and that these are badges of the Brotherhood of the Door."

Sturt, the helmsman, leaned toward the inspector. "We've rounded North Foreland, sir," he cried. "Head straight south along the coast," Campbell ordered. "Chandra Dass must have gone this way. No doubt he thinks he's shaken us off, and is making for the gathering-place of the Brotherhood, wherever that may be."

"The cutter isn't built for seas like this," Sturt said, shaking his head. "But I'll do it."

They were now following the coast southward, the lights of Ramsgate dropping back on their right. The waters out here in the Channel were wilder, great black waves tossing the cutter to the sky one moment, and then dropping it sickeningly the next. Frequently its screws raced loudly as they encountered no resistance but air.

Ennis, clinging precariously on the foredeck, turned the searchlight's stabbing white beam back and forth on the heaving dark sea ahead, but without any sign of their quarry disclosed.

White foam of breaking waves began to show around them like bared teeth, and there was a humming in the air.

"Storm coming up the Channel," Sturt exclaimed. "It'll do for us if it catches us out here."

"We've got to keep on," Ennis told him desperately. "We must come up with them soon!"

The coast on their right was now one of black, rocky cliffs, towering all along the shore in a jagged, frowning wall against which the waves dashed foamy white. The cutter crept southward over the wild waters, tossed like a chip upon the great waves. Sturt was having a hard time holding the craft out from the rocks, and had its prow pointed obliquely away from them.

The humming in the air changed to a shrill whistling as the outrider winds of the storm came upon them. The cutter tossed still more wildly and black masses of water smashed in upon them from the darkness, dazing and drenching them.

Suddenly Ennis yelled, "There's the lights of a boat ahead! There, moving in toward the cliffs!"

He pointed ahead, and Campbell and the helmsman peered through the blinding spray and darkness. A pair of low lights were moving at high speed on the waters there, straight toward the towering black cliffs. Then they vanished suddenly from sight.

"There must be a hidden opening or harbor of some kind in the cliffs!" Inspector Campbell exclaimed. "But that can't be Chandra Dass' boat, for it carried no lights."

"It might be others of the Brotherhood going to the meeting place!" Ennis exclaimed. "We can follow and see."

*S*turt thrust his head through the flying spray and shouted, "There are openings and water-caverns in plenty along these cliffs, but there's nothing in any of them."

"We'll find out," Campbell said. "Head straight toward the cliffs in there where that boat vanished."

"If we can't find the opening we'll be smashed to flinders on those cliffs," Sturt warned.

"I'm gambling that we'll find the opening," Campbell told him. "Go ahead."

Sturt's face set stolidly and he said, "Yes, sir."

He turned the prow of the cutter toward the cliffs. Instantly they dashed forward toward the rock walls with greatly increased speed, wild waves bearing them onward like charging stallions of the sea.

Hunched beside the helmsman, the searchlight stabbing the dark wildly as the cutter was flung forward by the waves, Ennis and the inspector watched as the cliffs loomed closer ahead. The brilliant white beam struck across the rushing, mountainous waves and showed only the towering barriers of rock, battered and smitten by the raving waters that frothed white. They could hear the booming thunder of the raging ocean striking the rock.

Like a projectile hurled by a giant hand, the cutter fairly flew now toward the cliffs. They now could see even the little streams that ran off the rough rock wall as each giant wave broke against it. They were almost upon it.

Sturt's face was deathly. "I don't see any opening!" he yelled. "And we're going to hit in a moment!"

"To your left!" screamed Inspector Campbell over the booming thunder. "There's an arched opening there."

Now Ennis saw it also, a huge archlike opening in the cliff that had been concealed by an angle of the wall. Sturt tried frantically to head the cutter toward it, but the wheel was useless as the great waves bore the craft along. Ennis saw they would strike a little to the side of the opening. The cliff loomed ahead, and he closed his eyes to the impact.

There was no impact. And as he heard a hoarse cry from Inspector Campbell, he opened his eyes.

The cutter was flying in through the mighty opening, snatched into it by powerful currents. They were whirled irresistibly forward under the huge rock arch, which loomed forty feet over their heads. Before them stretched a winding water-tunnel inside the cliff.

And now they were out of the wild uproar of the storming waters outside, and in an almost stupefying silence. Smoothly, resistlessly, the current bore them on in the tunnel, whose winding turns ahead were lit up by their searchlight.

"God, that was close!" exclaimed Inspector Campbell.

His eyes flashed. "Ennis, I believe that we have found the gathering-place of the Brotherhood. That boat we sighted is somewhere ahead in here, and so must be Chandra Dass, and your wife."

Ennis' hand tightened on his gun-butt. "If that's so — if we can just find them —"

"Blind action won't help if we do," said the inspector swiftly. "There must be all the number of the Brotherhood's members assembled here, and we can't fight them all."

His eyes suddenly lit and he took the blazing jeweled stars from his pocket. "These badges! With them we can pose as members of the Brotherhood, perhaps long enough to find your wife."

"But Chandra Dass will be there, and if he sees us —"

Campbell shrugged. "We'll have to take that chance. It's the only course open to us."

The current of the inflowing tide was still bearing them smoothly onward through the winding water-tunnel, around bends and angles where they scraped the rock, down long straight stretches. Sturt used the motors to guide them around the turns. Meanwhile, Inspector Campbell and Ennis quickly ripped from the cutter its police-insignia and covered all evidences of its being a police craft.

Sturt suddenly snicked off the searchlight. "Light ahead there!" he exclaimed.

Around the next turn of the water-tunnel showed a gleam of strange, soft light.

"Careful, now!" cautioned the inspector. "Sturt, whatever we do, you stay in the cutter. And try to have it ready for a quick getaway, if we leave it."

Sturt nodded silently. The helmsman's stolid face had become a little pale, but he showed no sign of losing his courage.

*T*he cutter sped around the next turn of the tunnel and emerged into a huge, softly lit cavern. Sturt's eyes bulged and Campbell uttered an exclamation of amazement. For in this mighty water-cavern there floated in a great mass, scores of sea-going craft, large and small.

All of them were capable of breasting storm and wind, and some were so large they could barely have entered. There were small yachts, big motor-cruisers, sea-going launches, cutters larger than their own, and among them the grey motor-launch of Chandra Dass.

They were massed together here, those with masts having lowered them to enter, floating and rubbing sides, quite unoccupied. Around the edges of the water-cavern ran a wide rock ledge. But no living person was visible and there was no visible source for the soft, strange white light that filled the astounding place.

"These craft must have come here from all over earth!" Campbell muttered. "The Brotherhood of the Door has assembled here — we've found their gathering-place all right."

"But where are they?" exclaimed Ennis. "I don't see anyone."

"We'll soon find out," the inspector said. "Sturt, run close to the ledge there and we'll get out on it."

Sturt obeyed, and as the cutter bumped the ledge, Campbell and Ennis leaped out onto it. They looked this way and that along it, but no one was in sight. The weirdness of it was unnerving, the strangely lit, mighty cavern, the assembled boats, the utter silence.

"Follow me," Campbell said in a low voice. "They must all be somewhere near."

He and Ennis walked a few steps along the ledge, when the American stopped. "Campbell, listen!" he whispered.

Dimly there whispered to them, as though from a distance and through great walls, a swelling sound of chanting. As they listened, hearts beating rapidly, a square of the rock wall of the cavern abruptly flew open beside them, as though hinged like a door. Inside it was the mouth of a soft-lit, man-high tunnel, and in its opening stood two men. They wore over their clothing shroudlike, loose-hanging robes of grey, asbestoslike material. They wore hoods of the same grey stuff over their heads, pierced with slits at the eyes and mouth. And each wore on his breast the blazing star-badge.

Through the eye-slits the eyes of the two surveyed Campbell and Ennis as they halted, transfixed by the sudden apparition. Then one of the hooded men spoke measuredly in a hissing, Mongolian voice.

"Are you who come here of the Brotherhood of the Door?" he asked, apparently repeating a customary challenge.

Campbell answered, his flat voice tremorless. "We are of the Brotherhood."

"Why do you not wear the badge of the Brotherhood, then?"

For answer, the inspector reached in his pocket for the strange emblem and fastened it to his lapel. Ennis did the same.

"Enter, brothers," said the hissing, hooded shape, standing aside to let them pass.

As they stepped into the tunnel, the hooded guard added in slightly more natural tones, "Brothers, you two are late. You must hurry to get your protective robes, for the ceremony soon begins."

Campbell inclined his head without speaking, and he and Ennis started along the tunnel. Its light, as sourceless as that of the great water-cavern, revealed that it was chiseled from solid rock and that it wound downward.

When they were out of sight of the two hooded guards, Ennis clutched the detective's arm convulsively.

"Campbell," he said, "the ceremony begins soon! We've got to find Ruth first!"

"We'll try," the inspector answered swiftly. "Those hooded robes are apparently issued to all the members to be worn during the ceremony as protection, for some reason, and once we get robes and get them on, Chandra Dass won't be able to spot us.

"Look out!" he added an instant later. "Here's the place where the robes are issued!"

The tunnel had debouched suddenly into a wider space in which were a group of men. Several were wearing the concealing hoods and robes, and one of these hooded figures was handing out, from a large rack of the robes, three of the garments to three dark Easterners who had apparently entered in the boat just ahead of the cutter.

The three dark Orientals, their faces gleaming with strange fanaticism, quickly donned the robes and hoods and passed hurriedly on down the tunnel. At once Campbell and Ennis stepped calmly up to the hooded custodians of the robes, and extended their hands.

One of the hooded figures took down two robes and handed them to them. But suddenly one of the other hooded men spoke sharply.

Instantly all the hooded men but the one who had spoken, with loud cries, threw themselves forward on Campbell and Paul Ennis.

Taken utterly by surprize, the two had no chance to draw their guns. They were smothered by grey-robed men, held helpless before they could move, a half-dozen pistols jammed into their bodies.

Stupefied by the sudden dashing of their hopes, the detective and the young American saw the hooded man who had spoken slowly lift the concealing grey cowl from his face. It was the dark, coldly contemptuous face of Chandra Dass.

IV

The Cavern of the Door

Chandra Dass spoke, and his strong, vibrant voice held a scorn that was almost pitying.

"It occurred to me that your enterprise might enable you to escape the daggers of my followers, and that you might trail us here," he said. "That is why I waited here to see if you came.

"Search them," he told the other hooded figures. "Take anything that looks like a weapon from them."

Ennis stared, stupefied, as the grey-hooded men obeyed. He was unable to believe entirely in the abrupt reversal of all their hopes, of their desperate attempt.

The hooded men took their pistols from Ennis and Campbell, and even the small gold knife attached to the chain of the inspector's big, old-fashioned gold watch. Then they stepped back, the pistols of two of them leveled at the hearts of the captives.

Chandra Dass had watched impassively. Ennis, staring dazedly, noted that the Hindu wore on his breast a different jewel-emblem from the others, a double star instead of a single one.

Ennis' dazed eyes lifted from the blazing badge to the Hindu's dark face. "Where's Ruth?" he asked a little shrilly, and then his voice cracked and he cried, "You damned fiend, where's my wife?"

"Be comforted, Mr. Ennis," came Chandra Dass' chill voice. "You are going now to join your wife, and to share her fate. You two are going with her and the other sacrifices through the Door when it opens. It is not usual," he added in cold mockery, "for our sacrificial victims to walk directly into our hands. We ordinarily have a more difficult time securing them."

He made a gesture to the two hooded men with pistols, and they ranged themselves close behind Campbell and Ennis.

"We are going to the Cavern of the Door," said the Hindu. "Inspector Campbell, I know and respect your resourcefulness. Be warned that your slightest attempt to escape means a bullet in your back. You two will march ahead of us," he said, and added mockingly, "Remember, while you live you can cling to the shadow of hope, but if these guns speak, it ends even that shadow."

Ennis and Inspector Campbell, keeping their hands elevated, started at the Hindu's command down the softly lit rock tunnel. Chandra Dass and the two hooded men with pistols followed.

Ennis saw that the inspector's sagging face was expressionless, and knew that behind that colorless mask, Campbell's brain was racing in an attempt to find a method of escape. For himself, the young American had almost forgotten all else in his eagerness to reach his wife. Whatever happened to Ruth, whatever mysterious horror lay in wait for her and the other victims, he would be there beside her, sharing it!

The tunnel wound a little further downward, then straightened out and ran straight for a considerable length. In this straight section of the rock passage, Ennis and Campbell for the first time perceived that the walls of the tunnel bore crowding, deeply chiseled inscriptions. They had not time to read them in passing, but Ennis saw that they were in many different languages, and that some of the characters were wholly unfamiliar.

"God, some of those inscriptions are in Egyptian hieroglyphics!" muttered Inspector Campbell.

The cool voice of Chandra Dass said, behind them, "There are pre-Egyptian inscriptions on these walls, inspector, could you but recognize them, carven in languages that perished from the face of earth before Egypt was born. Yes, back through time, back through mediæval and Roman and Egyptian and pre-Egyptian ages, the Brotherhood of the Door has existed and has each year gathered in this place to open the Door and worship with sacrifices They Beyond it."

The fanatic note of unearthly devotion was in his voice now, and Ennis shuddered with a cold not of the tunnel.

As they proceeded, they heard a muffled, hoarse booming somewhere over their heads, a dull, rhythmic thunder that echoed along the long passageway. The walls of the tunnel now were damp and glistening in the sourceless soft light, tiny trickles running down them.

"You hear the ocean over us," came Chandra Dass' voice. "The Cavern of the Door lies several hundred yards out from shore, beneath the rock floor of the sea."

They passed the dark mouths of unlit tunnels branching ahead from this illuminated one. Then over the booming of the raging sea above them, there came to Ennis' ears the distant, swelling chant they had heard in the water-cavern above. But now it was louder, nearer. At the sound of it, Chandra Dass quickened their pace.

Suddenly Inspector Campbell stumbled on the slippery rock floor and went down in a heap. Instantly Chandra Dass and his two followers recoiled from them, the two pistols trained on the detective as he scrambled up.

"Do not do that again, inspector," warned the Hindu in a deadly voice. "All tricks are useless now."

"I couldn't help slipping on this wet floor," complained Inspector Campbell.

"The next time you make a wrong step of any kind, a bullet will smash your spine," Chandra Dass told him. "Quick — march!"

*T*he tunnel turned sharply, turned again. As they rounded the turns, Ennis saw with a sudden electric thrill of hope that Campbell held clutched in his hand, concealed by his sleeve, the heel-hilted knife from his shoe. He had drawn it when he stumbled.

Campbell edged a little closer to the young American as they were hastening onward, and whispered to him, a word at a time.

"Be — ready — to jump — them —"

"But they'll shoot, your first move —" whispered Ennis agonizedly.

Campbell did not answer. But Ennis sensed the detective's body tautening.

They came to another turn, the strong, swelling chant coming loud from ahead. They started around that turn.

Then Inspector Campbell acted. He whirled as though on a pivot, the heel-knife flashing toward the men behind them.

Shots coughed from the pistols that were pressed almost against his stomach. His body jerked as the bullets struck it, yet he remained erect, his knife stabbing with lightning rapidity.

One of the hooded men slumped down with a pierced throat, and as Campbell sprang at the other, Ennis desperately launched himself at Chandra Dass. He bore the Hindu from his feet, but it was as though he was fighting a demon. Inside his grey robe, Chandra Dass writhed with fiendish strength.

Ennis could not hold him, the Hindu's body seeming of spring-steel. He rolled over, dashed the young American to the floor, and leaped up, his dark face and great black eyes blazing.

Then, halfway erect, he suddenly crumpled, the fire in his eyes dulling, a call for help smothered on his lips. He fell on his face, and Ennis saw that the heel-knife was stuck in his back. Inspector Campbell jerked it out, and put it back into his shoe. And now Ennis, staggering up, saw that Campbell had knifed the two hooded guards and that they lay in a dead heap.

"Campbell!" cried the American, gripping the detective's arm. "They've wounded you — I saw them shoot you."

Campbell's bruised face grinned briefly. "Nothing of the kind," he said, and tapped the soiled grey vest he wore beneath his coat. "Chandra Dass didn't know this vest is bullet-proof."

He darted an alert glance up and down the lighted tunnel. "We can't stay here or let these bodies lie here. They may be discovered at any moment."

"Listen!" said Ennis, turning.

The chanting from ahead swelled down the tunnel, louder than at any time yet, waxing and waxing, reaching a triumphant crescendo, then again dying away.

"Campbell, they're going on with the ceremony now!" Ennis cried. "Ruth!"

The detective's desperate glance fastened on the dark mouth of one of the branching tunnels, a little ahead.

"That side tunnel — we'll pull the bodies in there!" he exclaimed.

Taking the pistols of the dead men for themselves, they rapidly dragged the three bodies into the darkness of the unlit branching tunnel.

"Quick, on with two of these robes," rasped Inspector Campbell. "They'll give us a little better chance."

Hastily Ennis jerked the grey robe and hood from Chandra Dass' dead body and donned it, while Campbell struggled into one of the others. In the robes and concealing hoods, they could not be told from any other two members of the Brotherhood, except that the badge on Ennis' breast was the double star instead of the single one.

Ennis then spun toward the main, lighted tunnel, Campbell close behind him. They recoiled suddenly into the darkness of the branching way, as they heard hurrying steps out in the lighted passage. Flattened in the darkness against the wall, they saw several of the grey-hooded members of the Brotherhood hasten past them from above, hurrying toward the gathering-place.

"The guards and robe-issuers we saw above!" Campbell said quickly when they were passed. "Come on, now."

He and Ennis slipped out into the lighted tunnel and hastened along it after the others.

Boom of thundering ocean over their heads and rising and falling of the tremendous chanting ahead filled their ears as they hurried around the last turns of the tunnel. The passage widened, and ahead they saw a massive rock portal through whose opening they glimpsed an immense, lighted space.

Campbell and Ennis, two comparatively tiny grey-hooded figures, hastened through the mighty portal. Then they stopped. Ennis felt frozen with the dazing shock of it. He heard the detective whisper fiercely beside him.

"It's the Cavern, all right — the Cavern of the Door!"

*T*hey looked across a colossal rock chamber hollowed out beneath the floor of ocean. It was elliptical in shape, three hundred feet by its longer axis. Its black basalt sides, towering, rough-hewn walls, rose sheer and supported the rock ceiling which was the ocean floor, a hundred feet over their heads.

This mighty cathedral hewn from inside the rock of earth was lit by a soft, white, sourceless light like that in the main tunnel. Upon the floor of the cavern, in regular rows across it, stood hundreds on hundreds of human figures, all grey-robed and grey-hooded, all with their backs to Campbell and Ennis, looking across the cavern to its farther end. At that farther end was a flat daïs of black basalt upon which stood five hooded men, four wearing the blazing double-star on their breasts, the fifth, a triple-star. Two of them stood beside a cubical, weird-looking grey metal mechanism from which upreared a spherical web of countless fine wires, unthinkably intricate in their network, many of them pulsing with glowing force. The sourceless light of the cavern and the tunnel seemed to pulse from that weird mechanism.

Up from that machine, if machine it was, soared the black basalt wall of that end of the cavern. But there above the grey mechanism the rough wall had been carved with a great, smooth facet, a giant, gleaming black oval face as smooth as though planed and polished. Only, at the middle of the glistening black oval face, were carven deeply four large and wholly unfamiliar characters. As Ennis and Campbell stared frozenly across the awe-inspiring place, sound swelled from the hundreds of throats. A slow, rising chant, it climbed and climbed until the basalt roof above seemed to quiver to it, crashing out with stupendous effect, a weird litany in an unknown tongue. Then it began to fall.

Ennis clutched the inspector's grey-robed arm. "Where's Ruth?" he whispered frantically. "I don't see any prisoners."

"They must be somewhere here," Campbell said swiftly. "Listen —"

As the chant died to silence, on the daïs at the farther end of the cavern the hooded man who wore the triple-jeweled star stepped forward and spoke. His deep, heavy voice rolled out and echoed across the cavern, flung back and forth from wall to rocky wall.

"Brothers of the Door," he said, "we meet again here in the Cavern of the Door this year, as for ten thousand years past our forefathers have met here to worship They Beyond the Door, and bring them the sacrifices They love.

"A hundred centuries have gone by since first They Beyond the Door sent their wisdom through the barrier between their universe and ours, a barrier which even They could not open from their side, but which their wisdom taught our fathers how to open.

"Each year since then have we opened the Door which They taught us how to build. Each year we have brought them sacrifices. And in return They have given us of their wisdom and power. They have taught us things that lie hidden from other men, and They have given us powers that other men have not.

"Now again comes the time appointed for the opening of the Door. In their universe on the other side of it, They are waiting now to take the sacrifices which we have procured for them. The hour strikes, so let the sacrifices be brought."

As though at a signal, from a small opening at one side of the cavern a triple file of marchers entered. A file of hooded grey members of the Brotherhood flanked on either side a line of men and women who did not wear the hoods or robes. They were thirty or forty in number. These men and women were of almost all races and classes, but all of them walked stiffly, mechanically, staring ahead with unseeing, distended eyes, like living corpses.

"Drugged!" came Campbell's shaken voice. "They're all drugged, and don't know what is going on."

Ennis' eyes fastened on a small, slender girl with chestnut hair who walked at the end of the line, a girl in a straight tan dress, whose face was white, stiff, like those of the others.

"There's Ruth!" he exclaimed frantically, his cry muffled by his hood.

He plunged in that direction, but Campbell held him back.

"No!" rasped the inspector. "You can't help her by simply getting yourself captured!"

"I can at least go with her!" Ennis exclaimed. "Let me go!"

Inspector Campbell's iron grip held him. "Wait, Ennis!" said the detective. "You've no chance that way. That robe of Chandra Dass' you're wearing has a double-star badge like those of the men up there on the daïs. That means that as Chandra Dass you're entitled to be up there with them. Go up there and take your place as though you were Chandra Dass — with the hood on, they can't tell the difference. I'll slip around to that side door out of which they brought the prisoners. It must connect with the tunnels, and it's not far from the daïs. When I fire my pistol from there, you grab your wife and try to get to that door with her. If you can do it, we'll have a chance to get up through the tunnels and escape."

Ennis wrung the inspector's hand. Then, without further reply, he walked boldly with measured steps up the main aisle of the cavern, through the grey ranks to the daïs. He stepped up onto it, his heart racing. The chief priest, he of the triple-star, gave him only a glance, as of annoyance at his lateness. Ennis saw Campbell's grey figure slipping round to the side door.

The grey-hooded hundreds before him had paid no attention to either of them. Their attention was utterly, eagerly, fixed upon the stiff-moving prisoners now being marched up onto the daïs. Ennis saw Ruth pass him, her white face an unfamiliar, staring mask.

The prisoners were ranged at the back of the daïs, just beneath the great, gleaming black oval facet. The guards stepped back from them, and they remained standing stiffly there. Ennis edged a little toward Ruth, who stood at the end of that line of stiff figures. As he moved imperceptibly closer to her, he saw the two priests beside the grey mechanism reaching toward knurled knobs of ebonite affixed to its side, beneath the spherical web of pulsing wires.

The chief priest, at the front of the daïs, raised his hands. His voice rolled out, heavy, commanding, reverberating again through all the cavern.

V

The Door Opens

"*W*here leads the Door?" rolled the chief priest's voice.

Back up to him came the reply of hundreds of voices, muffled by the hoods but loud, echoing to the roof of the cavern in a thunderous response.

"It leads outside our world!"

The chief priest waited until the echoes died before his deep voice rolled on in the ritual.

"Who taught our forefathers to open the Door?"

Ennis, edging desperately closer and closer to the line of victims, felt the mighty response reverberate about him.

"They Beyond the Door taught them!"

Now Ennis was apart from the other priests on the daïs, within a few yards of the captives, of the small figure of Ruth.

"To whom do we bring these sacrifices?"

As the high priest uttered the words, and before the booming answer came, a hand grasped Ennis and pulled him back from the line of victims. He spun round to find that it was one of the other priests who had jerked him back.

"We bring them to Those Beyond the Door!"

As the colossal response thundered, the priest who had jerked Ennis back whispered urgently to him. "You go too close to the victims, Chandra Dass! Do you wish to be taken with them?"

The fellow had a tight grip on Ennis' arm. Desperate, tensed, Ennis heard the chief priest roll forth the last of the ritual.

"Shall the Door be opened that They may take the sacrifices?"

Stunning, mighty, a tremendous shout that mingled in it worshipping awe and superhuman dread, the answer crashed back.

"Let the Door be opened!"

The chief priest turned and his up-flung arms whirled in a signal. Ennis, tensing to spring toward Ruth, saw the two priests at the grey mechanism swiftly turn the knurled black knobs. Then Ennis, like all else in the vast cavern, was held frozen and spellbound by what followed.

The spherical web of wires pulsed up madly with shining force. And up at the center of the gleaming black oval facet on the wall, there appeared a spark of unearthly green light. It blossomed outward, expanded, an awful viridescent flower blooming quickly outward farther and farther. And as it expanded, Ennis saw that he could look *through* that green light! He looked through into another universe, a universe lying infinitely far across alien dimensions from our own, yet one that could be reached through this door between dimensions. It was a green universe, flooded with an awful green light that was somehow more akin to darkness than to light, a throbbing, baleful luminescence.

Ennis saw dimly through green-lit spaces a city in the near distance, an unholy city of emerald hue whose unsymmetrical, twisted towers and minarets aspired into heavens of hellish viridity. The towers of that city swayed to and fro and writhed in the air. And Ennis saw that here and there in the soft green substance of that restless city were circles of lurid light that were like yellow eyes.

In ghastly, soul-shaking apprehension of the utterly alien, Ennis knew that the yellow circles were *eyes* — that that hell-spawned city of another universe was *living* — that its unfamiliar life was single yet multiple, that its lurid eyes looked now through the Door!

Out from the insane living metropolis glided pseudopods of its green substance, glided toward the Door. Ennis saw that in the end of each pseudopod was one of the lurid eyes. He saw those eyed pseudopods come questing through the Door, onto the daïs.

The yellow eyes of light seemed fixed on the row of stiff victims, and the pseudopods glided toward them. Through the open door was beating wave on wave of unfamiliar, tingling forces that Ennis felt even through the protective robe.

The hooded multitude bent in awe as the green pseudopods glided toward the victims faster, with avid eagerness. Ennis saw them reaching for the prisoners, for Ruth, and he made a tremendous mental effort to break the spell that froze him. In that moment pistol-shots crashed across the cavern and a stream of bullets smashed the pulsing web of wires!

The Door began instantly to close. Darkness crept back around the edges of the mighty oval. As though alarmed, the lurid-eyed pseudopods of that hell-city recoiled from the victims, back through the dwindling Door. And as the Door dwindled, the light in the cavern was failing.

"Ruth!" yelled Ennis madly, and sprang forward and grasped her, his pistol leaping into his other hand.

"Ennis – quick!" shouted Campbell's voice across the cavern.

The Door dwindled away altogether; the great oval facet was completely black. The light was fast dying too.

The chief priest sprang madly toward Ennis, and as he did so, the hooded hordes of the Brotherhood recovered from their paralysis of horror and surged madly toward the daïs.

"The Door is closed! Death to the blasphemers!" cried the chief priest as he plunged forward.

"Death to the blasphemers!" shrieked the crazed horde below.

Ennis' pistol roared and the chief priest went down. The light in the cavern died completely at that moment.

In the dark a torrent of bodies catapulted against Ennis, screaming vengeance. He struck out with his pistol-barrel in the mad mêlée, holding Ruth's stiff form close with his other hand. He heard the other drugged, helpless victims crushed down and trampled under foot by the surging horde of vengeance-mad members.

*C*linging to the girl, Ennis fought like a madman through a darkness in which none could distinguish friend or foe, toward the door at the side from which Campbell had fired. He smashed down the pistol-barrel on all before him, as hands sought to grab him in the dark. He knew sickeningly that he was lost in the combat, with no sense of the direction of the door.

Then a voice roared loud across the wild din, "Ennis, this way! This way, Ennis!" yelled Inspector Campbell, again and again.

Ennis plunged through the whirl of unseen bodies in the direction of the detective's shouting voice. He smashed through, half dragging and half carrying the girl, until Campbell's voice was close ahead in the dark. He fumbled at the rock wall, found the door opening, and then Campbell's hands grasped him to pull him inside.

Hands grabbed him from behind, striving to tear Ruth from him, to jerk him back. Voices shrieked for help.

Campbell's pistol blazed in the dark and the hands released their grip. Ennis stumbled with the girl through the door into a dark tunnel. He heard Campbell slam a door shut, and heard a bar fall with a clang.

"Quick, for God's sake!" panted Campbell in the dark. "They'll follow us — we've got to get up through the tunnels to the water-cavern!"

They raced along the pitch-dark tunnel, Campbell now carrying the girl, Ennis reeling drunkenly along.

They heard a mounting roar behind them, and as they burst into the main tunnel, no longer lighted but dark like the others, they looked back and saw a flickering of light coming up the passage.

"They're after us and they've got lights!" Campbell cried. "Hurry!"

It was nightmare, this mad flight on stumbling feet up through the dark tunnels where they could hear the sea booming close overhead, and could hear the wild pursuit behind.

Their feet slipped on the damp floor and they crashed into the walls of the tunnel at the turns. The pursuit was closer behind — as they started climbing the last passages to the water-cavern, the torchlight behind showed them to their pursuers and wild yells came to their ears.

They had before them only the last ascent to the water-cavern when Ennis stumbled and went down. He swayed up a little, yelled to Campbell. "Go on — get Ruth out! I'll try to hold them back a moment!"

"No!" rasped Campbell. "There's another way — one that may mean the end for us too, but our only chance!"

The inspector thrust his hand into his pocket, snatched out his big, old-fashioned gold watch.

He tore it from its chain, turned the stem of it twice around. Then he hurled it back down the tunnel with all his force.

"Quick — out of the tunnels now or we'll die right here!" he yelled.

They lunged forward, Campbell dragging both the girl and the exhausted Ennis, and emerged a moment later into the great water-cavern. It was now lit only by the searchlight of their waiting cutter.

As they emerged into the cavern, they were thrown flat on the rock ledge by a violent movement of it under them. An awful detonation and thunderous crashing of falling rock smote their ears.

Following that first tremendous crash, giant rumbling of collapsing rock shook the water-cavern.

"To the cutter!" Campbell cried. "That watch of mine was filled with the most concentrated high-explosive known, and it's blown up the tunnels. Now it's touched off more collapses and all these caverns and passages will fall in on us at any moment!"

The awful rumbling and crashing of collapsing rock masses was deafening in their ears as they lurched toward the cutter. Great chunks of rock were falling from the cavern roof into the water.

*S*turt, white-faced but asking no questions, had the motor of the cutter running, and helped them pull the unconscious girl aboard.

"Out of the tunnel at once!" Campbell ordered. "Full speed!"

They roared down the water-tunnel at crazy velocity, the searchlight beam stabbing ahead. The tide had reached flood and turned, increasing the speed with which they dashed through the tunnel.

Masses of rock fell with loud splashes behind them, and all around them was still the ominous grinding of mighty weights of rock. The walls of the tunnel quivered repeatedly.

Sturt suddenly reversed the propellers, but in spite of his action the cutter smashed a moment later into a solid rock wall. It was a mass of rock forming an unbroken barrier across the water-tunnel, extending beneath the surface of the water.

"We're trapped!" cried Sturt. "A mass of the rock has settled here and blocked the tunnel."

"It can't be completely blocked!" Campbell exclaimed. "See, the tide still runs out beneath it. Our one chance is to swim out under the blocking mass of rock, before the whole cliff gives way!"

"But there's no telling how far the block may extend —" Sturt cried.

Then as Campbell and Ennis stripped off their coats and shoes, he followed their example. The rumble of grinding rock around them was now continuous and nerve-shattering.

Campbell helped Ennis lower Ruth's unconscious form into the water.

"Keep your hand over her nose and mouth!" cried the inspector. "Come on, now!"

Sturt went first, his face pale in the searchlight beam as he dived under the rock mass. The tidal current carried him out of sight in a moment.

Then, holding the girl between them, and with Ennis' hand covering her mouth and nostrils, the other two dived. Down through the cold waters they shot, and then the swift current was carrying them forward like a mill-race, their bodies bumping and scraping against the rock mass overhead.

Ennis' lungs began to burn, his brain to reel, as they rushed on in the waters, still holding the girl tightly. They struck solid rock, a wall across their way. The current sucked them downward, to a small opening at the bottom. They wedged in it, struggled fiercely, then tore through it. They rose on the other side of it into pure air. They were in the darkness, floating in the tunnel beyond the block, the current carrying them swiftly onward.

The walls were shaking and roaring frightfully about them as they were borne round the turns of the tunnel. Then they saw ahead of them a circle of dim light, pricked with white stars.

The current bore them out into that starlight, into the open sea. Before them in the water floated Sturt, and they swam with him out from the shaking, grinding cliffs.

The girl stirred a little in Ennis' grasp, and he saw in the starlight that her face was no longer dazed.

"Paul —" she muttered, clinging close to Ennis in the water.

"She's coming back to consciousness — the water must have revived her from that drug!" he cried.

But he was cut short by Campbell's cry. "Look! Look!" cried the inspector, pointing back at the black cliffs.

In the starlight the whole cliff was collapsing, with a prolonged, terrible roar as of grinding planets, its face breaking and buckling. The waters around them boiled furiously, whirling them this way and that.

Then the waters quieted. They found they had been flung near a sandy spit beyond the shattered cliffs, and they swam toward it.

"The whole underground honeycomb of caverns and tunnels gave way and the sea poured in!" Campbell cried. "The Door, and the Brotherhood of the Door, are ended forever!"

www.ingramcontent.com/pod-product-compliance
Lightning Source LLC
Chambersburg PA
CBHW030543180626
46810CB00005B/1980